Disney
MICKEY
& FRIENDS

we make books come alive™

 Phoenix International Publications, Inc.

Chicago • London • New York • Hamburg • Mexico City • Paris • Sydney

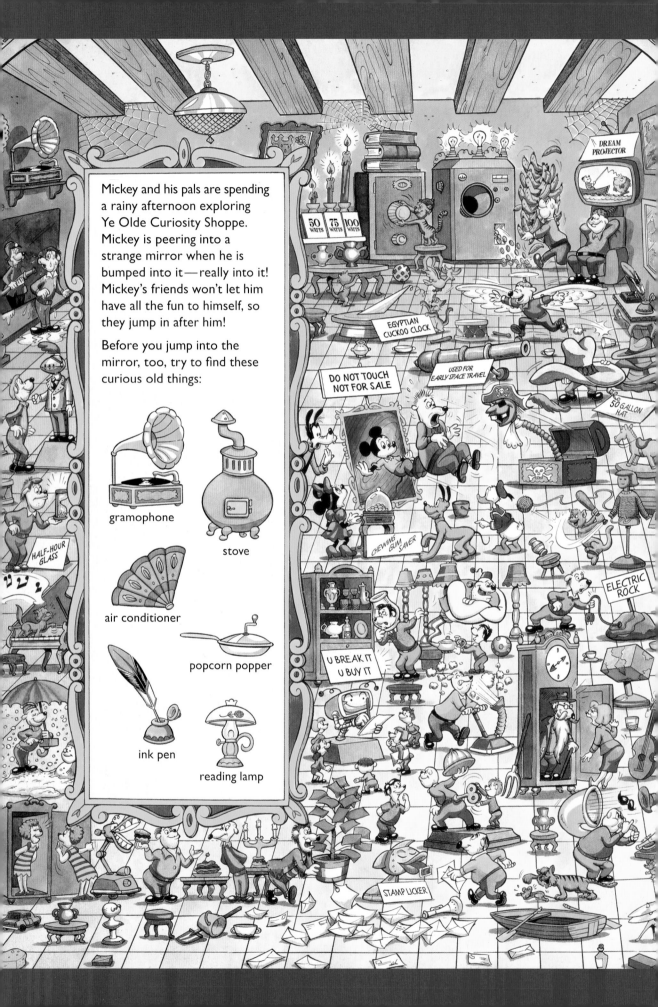

Mickey and his pals are spending a rainy afternoon exploring Ye Olde Curiosity Shoppe. Mickey is peering into a strange mirror when he is bumped into it—really into it! Mickey's friends won't let him have all the fun to himself, so they jump in after him!

Before you jump into the mirror, too, try to find these curious old things:

gramophone

stove

air conditioner

popcorn popper

ink pen

reading lamp

It's the year 2999, and Robo-Pete is cloning hundreds of naughty Mickeys, Minnies, Goofys, Donalds, and Plutos!

First, find the remote to turn off the Robo-Clone Machine. Then help the gang look for these Robo-Clones:

remote

Sprocket Mickey

Gyro Goofy

Submarine Donald

Rocket Minnie

Spring-Action Pluto

Next stop: Main Street, USA! The Saturday matinee just ended, and everyone is talking about the new movie, *Aliens from the Pistachio Planet.* Or *was* it a movie?

Good thing Mickey and his pals are on the scene to send these real space aliens home!

Can you find aliens in these flavors?

orange

vanilla

Neapolitan

mint chip

chocolate

peppermint

strawberry

Ahoy! Mickey is about to take a saltwater bath. Can his friends rescue him from his perilous perch? Or will Patch-Eye Pete and his scurvy seadogs make him walk the plank?

It's easy to spot Mickey, but can you find these pirates?

Slippery Sam

Brilliant Betsy

Hard-Headed Harry

Jolly Roger

Cue-Ball Bob

Pretty-Boy Lloyd

Pirate Peg

CASTAWAYS CHARTER CO.

Neptune Snacks Cove

WANTED

Mickey and the gang hop through the mirror again for a change of scenery. The Stone Age is lovely to look at, but not much is happening. Ugh! To get things "rocking," Mickey suggests a talent show.

Can you find these talented performers?

Ugga

Oop

Grunt

Oona

Eeeg

Gorp

When in Rome, do as the Romans do! That's Mickey's advice to his pals when they find themselves at Caesar's place. The gang is trying to blend in, but it's all Greek to them!

Can you find these Roman things?

XV
Roman numeral

goddess

this soldier

this toga

key

bathtub

Roman candle

PORTRAITS WHILE YOU WAIT

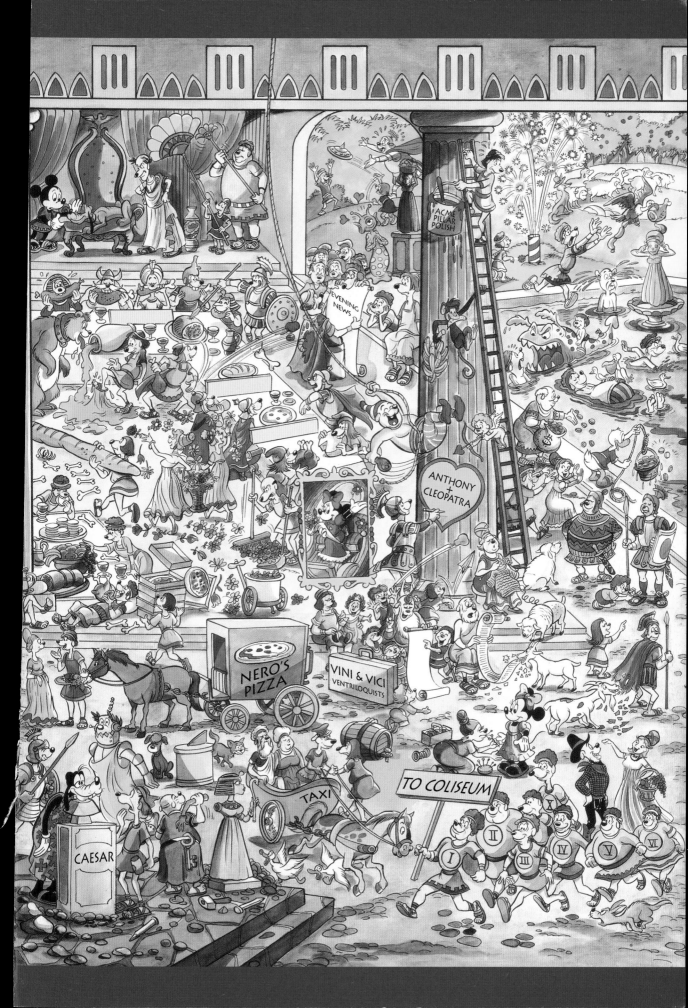

Go back to Ye Olde Curiosity Shoppe to find curious cats doing these things:

- ❏ wearing a hat
- ❏ fishing in a fishbowl
- ❏ painting a picture
- ❏ catching a mouse
- ❏ playing the piano
- ❏ cracking a safe
- ❏ reading a book
- ❏ unknitting a sweater

Go back to the future. Can you find these robo-citizens?

- ❏ robo-cop
- ❏ robo-doctor
- ❏ robo-chef
- ❏ robo-dogcatcher
- ❏ robo-ballerina
- ❏ robo-tennis player

Rock 'n' roll back to Main Street, USA! Can you find these nifty fifties things?

- ❏ poodle in a skirt
- ❏ hula hoop
- ❏ sock hopping
- ❏ real beehive hairdo
- ❏ jukebox
- ❏ saddle shoes
- ❏ rock and roll

Yo, ho, ho! A pirate's life is *not* for Mickey! Return to the ship to find these pirate things:

- ❏ treasure chest
- ❏ green parrot
- ❏ treasure map
- ❏ real crow's nest
- ❏ Long John's long johns
- ❏ blue beard
- ❏ crocodile

Get thee backe to Merrie Olde England. Canne ye finde these "knight" things?

- ❐ knight watch
- ❐ knight mare
- ❐ knight light
- ❐ knight crawler
- ❐ knight club

You. Stone Age. Back. Find rock things.

- ❐ rock 'n' roll band
- ❐ rock-a-bye baby
- ❐ rocking chair
- ❐ The Rock-ettes
- ❐ rock around the clock
- ❐ rocking the boat
- ❐ rock-et ship

Et tu, Mickey? Return to Caesar's time to find these people who hope to please the emperor:

- ❐ juggler
- ❐ fiddler
- ❐ clown
- ❐ ventriloquist
- ❐ chef
- ❐ painter

The fun isn't over! Go back to the heroes' parade to find these things honoring them:

- ❐ Mickey T-shirt
- ❐ Pluto beach towel
- ❐ Minnie poster
- ❐ Goofy TV special
- ❐ Donald flag
- ❐ extra edition of the newspaper
- ❐ key to the city